A TRIP TO THE BOTTOM OF THE WORLD

With Mouse

A TOON BOOK

By Frank Viva

Here
we are,
Mouse!

Oh...

For Mouse and all the other pets
I have had the pleasure to know.

Editorial Director: FRANÇOISE MOULY • Guest Editor: NADJA SPIEGELMAN

Book Design: FRANK VIVA and FRANÇOISE MOULY

FRANK VIVA's artwork was created using Adobe Illustrator. It is printed using 5 special inks on 140gsm smooth vellum paper.

The words are set in Neutraface, and the display type is hand drawn by Frank Viva.

 Printed in Dongguan, China, by Toppan Leefung.

The Library of Congress has cataloged the hardcover edition as follows:

Viva, Frank. • A trip to the bottom of the world with Mouse / Frank Viva. • p. cm. • Summary: A boy and a mouse take a bumpy sea journey to the majestic expanses of the Antarctic, where they see the sights and meet new friends. • ISBN 978-1-935179-19-1 • 1. Graphic novels. [1. Graphic novels. 2. Antarctica--Fiction. 3. Animals--Antarctica--Fiction. 4. Mice--Fiction.]

I. Title. • PZ7.7.V59Tr 2012 • 741.5'973--dc23 • 2011049499

ISBN: 978-1-935179-19-1 (hardcover) ISBN: 978-1-943145-23-2 (paperback)

17 18 19 20 21 22 TPN 10 9 8 7 6 5 4 3 2 1

www.TOON-BOOKS.com

Can we go **home** now?
Not yet, Mouse.

Wow! The waves go up...

and up...
and **UP**!
These waves make it hard to...

eat...

sleep...

kiss...

draw...

and stand!
Can we go
home now?

Not yet,
Mouse.

It is COLD out there, Mouse.

Then you will need...

boots...

mittens...

a hat...

a scarf...

and a
snowsuit!
Can we go
home now?

Not yet,
Mouse.

I want to go home now.
Why, Mouse? Look at the ***big*** sky! It makes me feel ***as small as***...

a tack?
a ladybug?
a seed?
a guppy?

Ohhh!
A mouse.

Yes, Mouse!
And I *like* small.

Can we
go home
now?

Not yet,
Mouse,
I see...

a yellow-eyed penguin...
a fairy penguin...

a macaroni penguin...
a king penguin...

and a
MOUSE?
WHAT?!

Can we
go home
NOW?

Not yet,
Mouse!

LOOK!
What is
THAT?

It's a whale!
Whales love
to...

jump...

bump...

play...

dive and...

SPLASH!

Can we go home ***now***?

70HP

Not yet! The water is **warm** here. Let's swim and maybe we'll see...

a jellyfish?
a seal?

a fish?

or a
starfish!

SWIMMING IS *FUN!*
Now can we go home?

Yes,
Mouse.

ABOUT THE AUTHOR

FRANK VIVA is an illustrator and designer who lives in Toronto, Canada. In addition to regularly creating cover art for *The New Yorker*, he is the author of several picture books including *Along a Long Road*, which was chosen by *The New York Times* as one of its best illustrated children's books. His other book for TOON, *Sea Change*, is a stunning novel that mixes graphics and text to tell a coming-of-age story set in Nova Scotia.

A Trip to the Bottom of the World is based on Frank's experiences aboard a Russian research vessel during a trip to the Antarctic Peninsula. On this once-in-a-lifetime adventure, while crossing the Drake Passage (the roughest waters in the world), he became sick—over and over and over again. But it was worth it. Once in Antarctica, he saw penguins and whales, and even swam in the thermal waters of a submerged volcano. This chronicle of Frank's journey was just as fun to do—and much easier on his tummy.

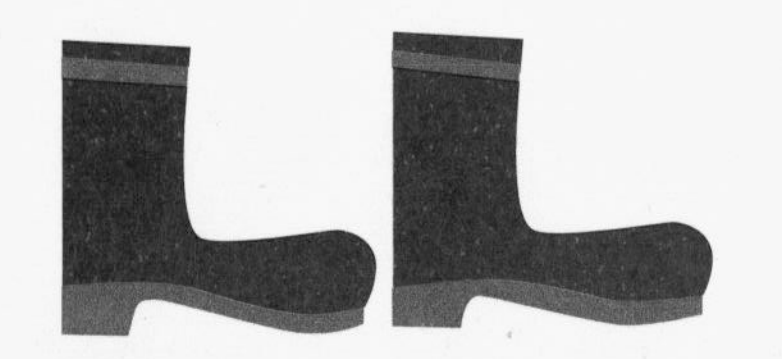

Are we there yet?

Not yet, Mouse.